D1220193

Illustrator Contact Information:

Dasia Doodles • Email address: dasiadoodles@gmail.com

Instagram Information: @dasiadoodles

Author Contact Information

Lauren Evans • lovebeyondwordsmovement@gmail.com

THE CAT CALLED TIGER

FACING YOUR FEARS

Dedication

This book is dedicated to Mr. Lawrence Evans Sr; a man whom I am proud to call my father. He has encouraged me through many obstacles in life and has given me hope when life has thrown many curve balls my way. I would often allow fear to hold me back from pursuing numerous ideas and visions that I had. Dad, I thank you for being my strength, my rock and my support system. Often you would call me and remind me of my successes before even saying hello on the phone. You have played a vital role in my life and in many of my accomplishments. I dedicate this book to you. Love you always!

A special thanks to my siblings: my twin brother Larry Evans, brother Lawrence Evans Jr. & sister Sherry Hunter.
We have gone through many hard times together and survived. Those moments have strengthened a bond among us. I am grateful for your support and friendship. Moreover, I'm proud to call you family.

In Loving Memory

Mrs. Shirley Ann Evans was a great mother. My life forever changed when she transitioned on May 27th , 2017. Losing my mother was one of the hardest battles that I was unprepared to face. My mom would often tell people that I was her, "Hard Rock or Doctor." She inspired me to pursue my Doctorate degree before she passed. I know she would be proud of how close I am to finishing my program. Thank you mom for the inspiration.

Preface

Have you ever dreamed of doing something great? Fear often prevents us from seeing the final product. Imagine if, at a young age, you had the power to overcome fear. Kids are often told, "You can be anything you want to be." But, they lack the blueprint for getting those things done.

This book is about a cat named Tiger. He is different from all the other cats. He is small, but his heart is big. He doesn't fear cats, dogs or spiders. This book will show you how a small and seemingly insignificant cat was able to accomplish something great.

Tiger wants to let children know (and even remind adults) that whatever fears you have, or had to overcome, not to let it stop you from being the hero that you were born to be.

When Tiger was born, he was the smallest kitten in his family.

Size didn't stop him.
He was a curious kitten.

Ellen, the farmer's little girl, came to the barn everyday. She cuddled all five kittens.

But, she always spent more time with Tiger. One day she said...

As Tiger grew, he remembered the little girl's words.

He jumped on big spiders

His Brothers and sisters often told him "You are a silly cat, Tiger. You don't know how to stay away from dangerous things"

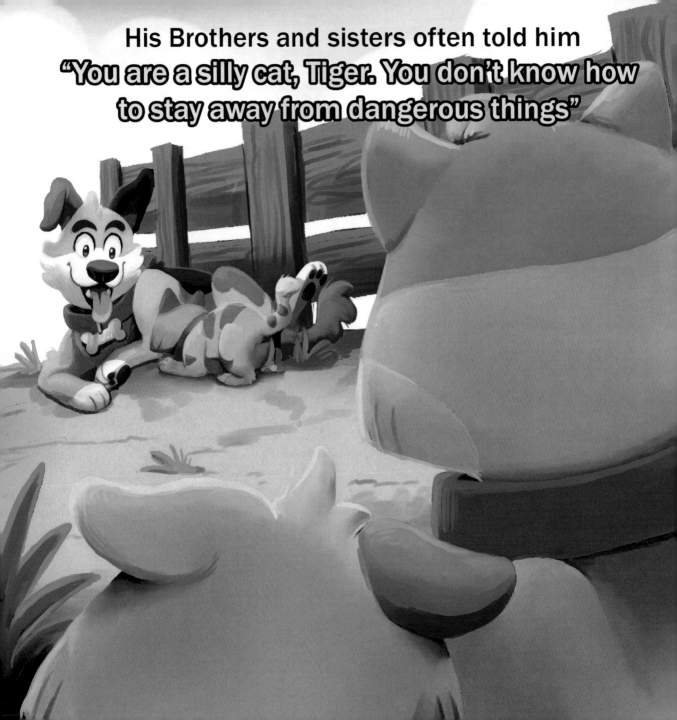

One night, Tiger smelled smoke...

Oh no! There's a fire in the shed! Look at all of the flames..!

Wake up! The shed is on fire. We need to get out, now!

Tiger's mother, brothers and sisters were afraid.
"We can't get out, it's too dangerous!" They cried.

But Tiger wouldn't let danger stop him.

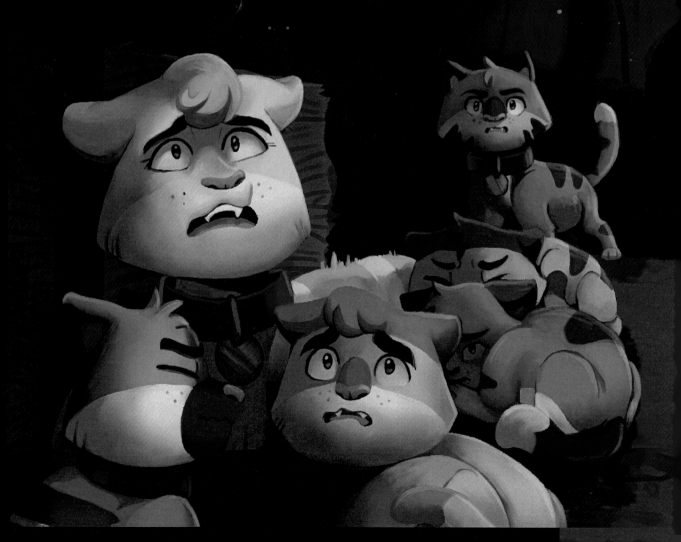

Follow me! I know the way out!

So, Tiger's mother and siblings followed him out of the burning shed.

Make your own Characters!

Create your own family of barnyard cats and dogs just like Tiger's! Don't be afraid to use any colors you want, and have fun!

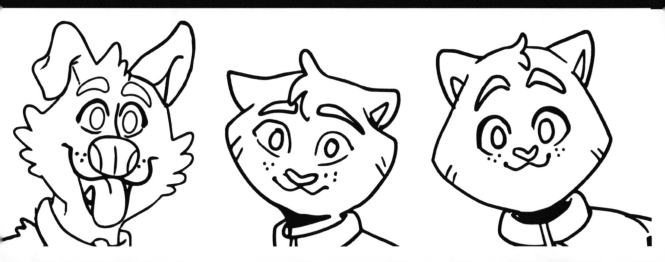

Meow! My name is:

_____

- - - - - - - - - - - - - - - - - -

_____

Meow! My name is:

Meow! My name is:

Meow! My name is:

Meow! My name is:

_____

- - - - - - - - - - - - - - - - - -

_____

Meow! My name is:

Woof! My name is:

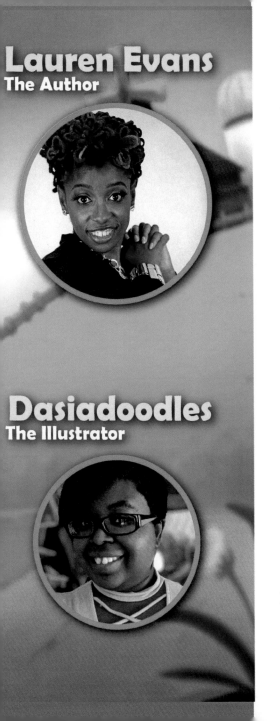

Lauren Evans
The Author

Dasiadoodles
The Illustrator

One day, while attending Serenity Pastoral Counseling, a therapy group run by Pamela Bell, I received a vision to write this book. Ms. Bell posed a question, "If I could say something to my childhood self, what would it be?" I was unable to answer the question at that time. I was full of anger having lost my mom and all the grief that comes with such a loss. When I was able to answer the question, I would have told my younger self that you do not have to be afraid. If it had not been for the Serenity Pastoral Counseling group, this book would not exist. This was a healing project for me. I was able to revisit my childhood creativity. With the help of my wonderful illustrator, I was able to create a powerful message for children all over the world on overcoming fear. If you can learn to overcome your fears at a young age, then you can accomplish great things.

lovebeyondwordsmovement@gmail.com

This illustrator is a Graphic Designer who is hilarious and hard working. She has a passion for visual storytelling and is gifted in making words come alive through art. You can find examples of her other works on:

Instagram **@dasiadoodles**

Made in United States
North Haven, CT
01 October 2022

24839465R00018